JACK

TOMIE dePAOLA

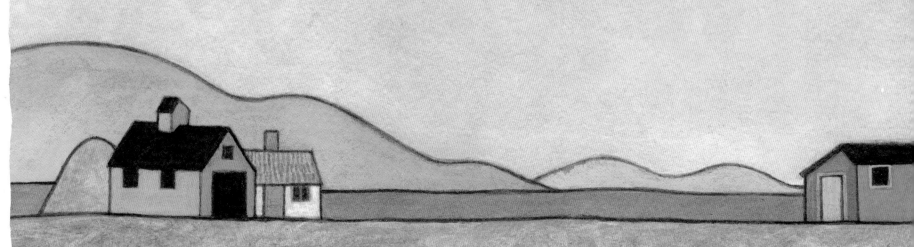

Nancy Paulsen Books ⟳ An Imprint of Penguin Group (USA)

This is a story about Jack.

FOR
MY FRIEND
PHILIP
PULLMAN,
WHO DRAWS,
AND CARVES,
AND WRITES
WONDERFUL
BOOKS.
TdeP·NH

Jack lived with his grandpa
on a tiny farm way out
in the country.

One day, Jack said, "Grandpa, I want to see the world and make new friends and live in a house in the city. How do I do it?"

"Why don't you go to the city and ask the king? I hear he is a wise and generous man. Maybe he can help you," said Grandpa.

So Jack put on his new shoes and set off.

On his way, Jack met a chick.

"Where are you going?" asked the chick.

"I'm going to the city to ask the king for a house," answered Jack.

"Can I come too?"

"Yes, please do."

Jack met a duck.

"We're going to the city to ask the king for a house," answered Jack.

"Can I come too?"

Jack met a goose and a dog.

"Where are you going?"
asked the goose and the dog.

"We're going to the city to ask the king for a house," answered Jack.

"Can we come too?"

"Yes, please do."

Jack met a frog, a pig, and a cow.

"Where are you going?"
asked the frog, the pig, and the cow.

"We're going to the city to ask the king for a house," answered Jack.

"Can we come too?"

"Yes, please do."

Jack met a cat, a sheep, a horse, and an owl.

"Where are you going?"
they all asked.

"We're going to the city to ask the king for a house," answered Jack.

"There seems to be a lot of you," said the owl, "but can we come too?"

"Yes, please do."

When they got to the city,
they went right to the king's castle.

"We're here to see the king," Jack said.

"Go right in," said the guard.

"Good afternoon, King," Jack said. "My friends and I would like to live in the city. Can you please help us find a house?"

"I heard you were coming," said the king. "I happen to have a nice, big house that would be perfect for all of you. It might need some fixing up, but I know you can do it."

"Oh, thank you," said Jack and his friends.
"We'll take it!"

And the king handed Jack the key.

"My dream has come true," said Jack.

"Ours too," chimed in Jack's friends.

"Look at that house!
There goes the neighborhood,"
the old man grumbled.

"And it's about TIME!"
chuckled the old woman.